This
Treasure Cove Story
belongs to

PINOCCHIO

A CENTUM BOOK 978-1-912396-16-0
Published in Great Britain by Centum Books Ltd.
This edition published 2018.

3 5 7 9 10 8 6 4 2

Centum Books Ltd, 20 Devon Square, Newton Abbot,
Devon, TQ12 2HR, UK.

www.centumbooksltd.co.uk | books@centumbooksltd.co.uk
CENTUM BOOKS Limited Reg.No. 07641486.

A CIP catalogue record for this book is available
from the British Library.

Printed in China.

centum

A Treasure Cove Story

WALT DISNEY'S

Pinocchio

Story adapted by Steffi Fletcher
Illustrated by Al Dempster

Digital scanning and restoration services provided
by Tim Lewis of Disney Publishing Worldwide
and Ron Stark of S/R Labs

One O ne night, the Evening Star shone down
on a tiny village. Only one house still had
a light burning and that was the workshop
of Geppetto, the kindly old woodcarver.
He was busy carving a little puppet.

'Isn't Pinocchio almost like a real
boy?' he chuckled.

Geppetto

Climbing into bed, the old man mumbled,
'I wish you were a real boy, Pinocchio.'
Jiminy Cricket overheard Geppetto's wish.
He had seen how kind and gentle the woodcarver
was, and he felt sorry because the lonely old
man's wish could never come true.

Suddenly a shimmering light filled the room.
Then a beautiful lady dressed in shining blue
appeared. She raised her wand and said…

'Wake, Pinocchio! Skip and run! Good Geppetto needs a son!' Pinocchio blinked his eyes and raised his wooden arms.

'I can move!' he cried. 'I'm a real boy!'

'No,' the Blue Fairy said sadly. 'You have life, but to become a real boy, you must prove yourself brave, truthful and unselfish.'

And Jiminy Cricket would help.

The next morning, Geppetto couldn't believe his eyes. There was his puppet, laughing and talking and running!

'It's true, Father!' Pinocchio cried. 'I'm alive!'

After the initial joy was over, Geppetto said, 'But now, Pinocchio, you must go to school. Study hard! Then you'll soon become a real boy!'

Meanwhile, Jiminy Cricket had overslept
and now jumped up in a great hurry. He caught
up with Pinocchio just as the silly little puppet
was walking off with the worst pair of scoundrels
in the whole countryside – J Worthington
Foulfellow and Gideon.

The villains convinced Pinocchio
that he should forget about school
and become an actor.

'But, Pinoke!' cried Jiminy. 'What will your father say?'

Pinocchio said, 'Father will be proud of me!'

Soon they came to a marionette theatre. When its owner, Stromboli, saw Pinocchio, his small, evil eyes glistened. 'What a drawing card!' he exclaimed. 'A puppet without strings!'

The fox nodded. 'And he's yours,' he said, smiling greedily and holding out his paw, 'for a certain price, of course!'

That night Pinocchio sang and danced.
The audience cheered for more. A puppet
without strings! It was a miracle!

But when Pinocchio started to head
home for the night, Stromboli snarled at him.
'You're mine, and you stay here!' And
bang! Before Pinocchio could resist,
he was locked in a birdcage!

'Oh, Jiminy,' Pinocchio sobbed, 'why didn't I go to school? I'll never see my father again!'

Suddenly the Blue Fairy appeared before the sad friends.

'I'll help you this time,' she said, 'because you are truly sorry. Run home now, Pinocchio, and be a good son, or you'll never become a real boy!'

'Whew!' Pinocchio sighed thankfully.
'Let's go home!'

He and Jiminy started running as fast
as they could, but whom should they bump
into but Foulfellow and Gideon!

This time Foulfellow persuaded the
gullible puppet to forget his good resolutions
and take a 'rest cure' on Pleasure Island.

'You promised to go right home!' Jiminy cried.
'But Foulfellow says I need a rest after
my terrible experience,' replied Pinocchio.
They came to a coach bound for
Pleasure Island. It was pulled by small donkeys
and filled with noisy boys. As Pinocchio
climbed aboard, Jiminy saw the evil-looking
coachman slip Foulfellow a heavy bag.
Again the fox had sold Pinocchio!

After boarding a ferry, the coach docked at
Pleasure Island. Here streets were paved with cookies
and fountains spouted lemonade.

Pinocchio soon made friends with a young bully
called Lampwick who was always in the middle
of mischief.

Jiminy was not happy. He shouted at the puppet
to go home.

'Don't tell me you're scared of a beetle!' Lampwick
snickered.

Jiminy was about to march off when all of a sudden
Lampwick and Pinocchio groaned.

The boys were sprouting donkey ears!
'It's donkey fever,' whispered Jiminy,
horrified. 'You were lazy, good-for-nothing
boys, so you're turning into donkeys!'
They quickly dashed through the streets.
As they rounded a corner, they saw the
coachman herding a bunch of braying donkeys,
many of which still wore boys' hats and shoes.

TO THE SALT MINES

Pinocchio and Jiminy managed to
climb up the wall surrounding the island,
but Lampwick had already turned into
a donkey.

There was nothing they could do.
With a lump in his throat, Pinocchio
followed Jiminy and dived into the sea
to escape.

They had a long, hard journey home.
By the time they came to the village, it was
winter. They hurried to Geppetto's door and
pounded on it. But the house was empty!

Just then a gust of wind blew a piece
of paper around the corner.

'Hey, Pinoke!' Jiminy exclaimed. 'It's a letter!'

Dear Pinocchio,

I heard you had gone to Pleasure Island, so Figaro,
Cleo and I started off in a small boat to find you.
Just as we came in sight of the island, out of the sea
rose Monstro, the giant whale. He opened his jaws;
in we went. Now, dear son, we are living in the
belly of the whale. But there is very little to eat
here, and we cannot exist much longer, so I fear
you will never again see your loving father.

Geppetto

For a while, they were both silent, too sad
to speak. Then Pinocchio stood tall and said,
'I am going to save my father!'

Just then a dove wearing a golden crown
appeared. 'I will take you,' she said. 'Climb on.'
Then she spread her wings and flew and flew
until they reached the seashore.

Pinocchio and Jiminy did not know
that the dove was the Blue Fairy in disguise
and that it was she who had brought them
Geppetto's letter.

When the dove was out of sight, Pinocchio
tied a big stone to his donkey tail. Then he and
Jiminy leaped off the cliff into the ocean below.

As soon as they reached the sandy bottom,
Pinocchio scrambled to his feet. 'Come on,'
he said. 'Let's find Monstro.'

'We'll never find him,' muttered Jiminy.
'We're probably looking in the wrong ocean!'

Jiminy was wrong. Very near them floated the whale they were looking for, fast asleep. Inside the whale was Geppetto. He had set up a crude home from the ships the whale had swallowed and every day he fished in the whale's belly. But now that Monstro was sleeping, no fish came in.

'Not a bite for days, Figaro,' Geppetto said mournfully to his cat. 'If Monstro doesn't wake soon, we'll all starve.'

Just then Geppetto felt a nibble. 'Food, Figaro!'
he cried. But when the catch was landed, it was
only a cookbook called *How to Cook Fish*.
It was a solemn moment. All felt that the
end was near. And then the whale moved!

Monstro gave an upward lunge and
through his jaws rushed a wall of water.
With it came fish – a whole school of tuna!
Pinocchio saw Monstro coming
at him. He held on to a fish and was
eaten, too.

Soon Geppetto was pulling fish after fish
out of the water. He was so busy, he almost
didn't notice Pinocchio getting pulled on board.
'Oh, my own dear son!' he exclaimed.
'Is it really you?'
They were thrilled to see each other again.
Now if they could only get out of the whale!
Pinocchio had a plan.

The puppet set fire to a pile of crates. As the fire
began to smoke, they jumped onto a raft. Soon the
whale gave a monstrous SNEEZE!

Out went the raft, past those crunching jaws, into
the open sea!

But they were not yet free. The angry whale plunged
after them and splintered their frail craft.

Geppetto was sinking. 'My son, save yourself!'
he cried.

But the brave puppet kept him afloat as giant
waves swept them toward the shore.

Geppetto lay on the beach, gratitude filling his
heart. And then he saw Pinocchio lying beside him,
still, cold and pale! The old man was heartbroken.

Geppetto gathered poor Pinocchio into his arms and headed home. Then he prayed.

Suddenly a ray of starlight appeared. A soft voice said, 'And someday, when you have proven yourself brave, truthful and unselfish, you will be a real boy…'

Pinocchio sat up. He looked at himself and felt his arms and legs. Then he knew!

'Father! Look at me!' he cried joyfully.

The Blue Fairy's promise had come true! Pinocchio was a real, live boy!

Treasure Cove Stories

1 Three Little Pigs
2 Snow White and
The Seven Dwarfs
3 The Fox and the Hound
- Hide-and-Seek
4 Dumbo
5 Cinderella
6 Cinderella's Friends
7 Alice in Wonderland
8 Mad Hatter's Tea Party
from Alice in Wonderland
9 Mickey Mouse and
his Spaceship
10 Peter Pan
11 Pinocchio
12 The Prince and the Pauper
13 Sleeping Beauty
and the Good Fairies
14 The Lucky Puppy
15 Chicken Little
16 Santa's Toy Shop
17 Coco
18 Winnie-the-Pooh
and Tigger
19 The Sword in the Stone
20 Mary Poppins
21 The Jungle Book
22 The Aristocats
23 Lady and the Tramp
24 Bambi
25 Bambi - Friends of the Forest
26 Pete's Dragon
27 Beauty and the Beast
- The Teapot's Tale
28 Monsters, Inc.
- M is for Monster
29 Finding Nemo
30 The Incredibles
31 The Incredibles
- Jack-Jack Attack
32 Ratatouille
- Your Friend the Rat
33 Wall·E
34 Up
35 Princess and the Frog
36 Toy Story - The Pet Problem
37 Dora the Explorer
- Dora and the Unicorn King

38 Dora the Explorer
- Grandma's House
39 Spider-Man
- Night of the Vulture!
40 Wreck-it Ralph
41 Brave
42 The Invincible Iron Man
- Eye of the Dragon
43 SpongeBob SquarePants
- Sponge in Space!
44 SpongeBob SquarePants
- Where the Pirates Arrrgh!
45 Toy Story
- A Roaring Adventure
46 Cars - Deputy Mater
Saves the Day!
47 Spider-Man
- Trapped By The Green Goblin!
48 Big Hero 6
49 Spider-Man - High Voltage!
50 Frozen
51 Cinderella Is My Babysitter
52 Beauty and the Beast
- I Am The Beast
53 Blaze and the Monster
Machines - Mighty Monster
Machines
54 Blaze and the Monster
Machines - Dino Parade!
55 Teenage Mutant Ninja Turtles
- Follow The Ninja!
56 I Am A Princess
57 Paw Patrol
- The Big Book of Paw Patrol
58 Paw Patrol
- Adventures with Grandpa!
59 Merida Is Our Babysitter
60 Trolls
61 Trolls Holiday Special
62 The Secret Life of Pets
63 Zootropolis
64 Ariel Is My Babysitter
65 Inside Out
66 Belle Is My Babysitter
67 The Lion Guard
- Eye In The Sky
68 Moana
69 Finding Dory

70 Guardians of the Galaxy
71 Captain America
- High-Stakes Heist!
72 Ant-Man
73 The Mighty Avengers
74 The Mighty Avengers
- Lights Out!
75 The Incredible Hulk
76 Shimmer & Shine
- Wish upon a Sleepover
77 Shimmer & Shine
- Backyard Ballet
78 Paw Patrol - All-Star Pups!
79 Teenage Mutant Ninja Turtles
- Really Spaced Out!
80 Cars 2 - Travel Buddies
81 Madagascar
82 Jasmine Is My Babysitter
83 How To Train Your Dragon
84 Shrek
85 Puss In Boots
86 Kung Fu Panda
87 Beauty and the Beast
- I Am Belle
88 The Lion Guard
- The Imaginary Okapi
89 Thor - Thunder Strike!
90 Guardians of the Galaxy
-Rocket to the Rescue!
91 Nella The Princess Knight
- Nella and the Dragon
92 Shimmer & Shine
- Treasure Twins!
93 Olaf's Frozen Adventure
94 Black Panther
95 Branch's Bunker Birthday
96 Shimmer & Shine
- Pet Talent Show
97 The Ugly Duckling
98 Look Out for Mater!
99 101 Dalmatians
100 The Sorcerer's Apprentice
101 Tangled
102 Vampirina
- The Littlest Vampire
103 Puppy Dog Pals
- Don't Rain on my Pug-Rade

Book list may be subject to change.